Dick and Jane

READING COLLECTION • VOLUME 1

We Look

GROSSET & DUNLAP • NEW YORK

Look

Look, look.

Oh, oh, oh.

Oh, oh.

Oh, look.

Jane

Oh, Jane.

Look, Jane, look.

Look, look.

Oh, look.

See Jane.

See, see.

See Jane.

Oh, see Jane.

Dick

Look, Jane.
Look, look.
See Dick.

See, see.

Oh, see.

See Dick.

Oh, see Dick.

Oh, oh, oh.

Funny, funny Dick.

Sally

Look, Dick.

Look, Jane.

See Sally.

Oh, oh, oh.

Oh, Dick.

See Sally.

Look, Jane.

Look, Dick.

See funny Sally.

Funny, funny Sally.

Big and Little

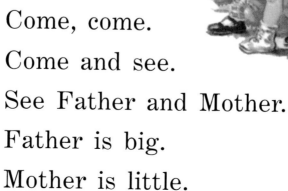

Come, come.

Come and see.

See Father and Mother.

Father is big.

Mother is little.

Look, Father.

Dick is big.

Sally is little.

Big, big Dick.

Little Baby Sally.

Oh, look, Jane.

Look, Dick, look.

Sally is big.

Tim is little.

Big, big Sally.

Little Baby Tim.

The Funny Baby

Come down, Dick.

Come and see.

See the big, big mother.

See the funny little baby.

Puff is my baby.

Puff is my funny little baby.

I see the big mother.
I see the little baby.
Look, Jane.
See the big father.

Look, Dick, look.

See something funny.

See my baby jump.

See my baby run.

Oh, oh, oh.

Something Blue

Oh, Jane, I see something.

I see something blue.

Come and see Mother work.

Mother can make something.

Something blue.

Look Mother, look.

I can work.

I can make something.

I can make something yellow.

Look, look.

See something yellow.